MORE TH

AN FLUFF

Madeline Valentine

Alfred A. Knopf ✧ New York

Daisy happened to be very fluffy.

Being fluffy was all anyone
noticed about her.

They squeezed her.

They petted her.

They kissed her.

They popped up out of nowhere
and tried to hug her.

It ruffled Daisy's feathers.

Only back at home could Daisy relax.

What about a smooch?

Something had to change.

Daisy decided the time
was right for a new look.

It was spectacular.

But it was also pretty icky . . .

a bit sticky . . .

and super-stinky.

By the end of the day, Daisy was right back where she started.

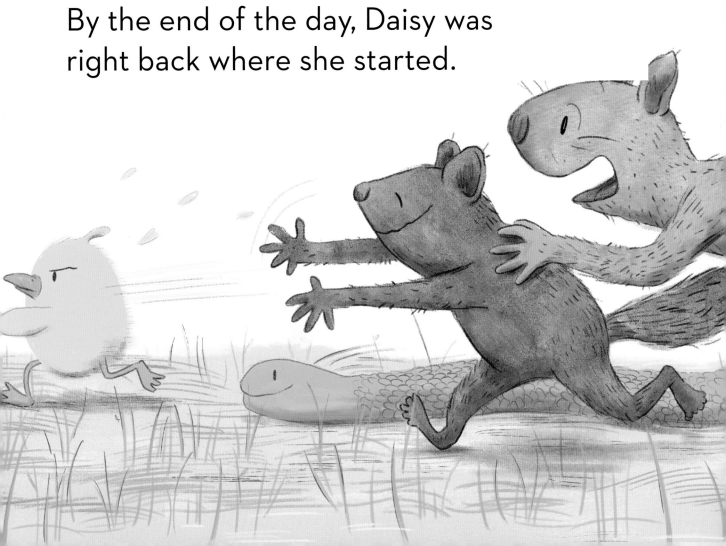

Daisy couldn't take
it anymore.

I AM MORE THAN FLUFF!

Mom decided to have a talk.

Daisy, honey.

I know you're angry,
but you cannot peck others.

But everybody cuddles me
when I don't want them to!

Daisy hatched
a plan.

But I wouldn't mind
a wing bump instead.

With a little practice, Daisy got the hang of letting everyone know what she wanted.

Everyone learned to give Daisy some space when she wanted it. And she did the same for them.

Daisy happened to be fluffy.
And that suited her just fine.

Would you like me to read you a story before bed.

For Rebecca Sherman,
strong chick and
super agent

THIS IS A BORZOI BOOK PUBLISHED BY ALFRED A. KNOPF

Copyright © 2021 by Madeline Valentine

All rights reserved. Published in the United States by Alfred A. Knopf, an imprint of Random House Children's Books,
a division of Penguin Random House LLC, New York.

Knopf, Borzoi Books, and the colophon are registered trademarks of Penguin Random House LLC.

Visit us on the Web! rhcbooks.com
Educators and librarians, for a variety of teaching tools, visit us at RHTeachersLibrarians.com

Library of Congress Cataloging-in-Publication Data
Names: Valentine, Madeline, author, illustrator.
Title: More than fluff / by Madeline Valentine.
Description: First edition. | New York : Alfred A. Knopf, 2021. | Audience: Ages 3–7. |
Audience: Grades K–1. | Summary: Daisy the chick is cute, fluffy, soft, and tired of others hugging
and petting her, so her mother suggests she tell them what she would prefer, such as a wing bump or a pinkie shake.
Identifiers: LCCN 2019056146 (print) | LCCN 2019056147 (ebook)
ISBN 978-0-593-17905-5 (hardcover) | ISBN 978-0-593-17906-2 (library binding) | ISBN 978-0-593-17907-9 (ebook)
Subjects: CYAC: Personal space—Fiction. | Friendship—Fiction. | Chickens—Fiction. | Animals—Infancy—Fiction.
Classification: LCC PZ7.V25214 Mor 2021 (print) | LCC PZ7.V25214 | (ebook) | DDC [E]—dc23

The text of this book is set in 25-point Neutraface.
The illustrations were created using digitally composed graphite and watercolor.

MANUFACTURED IN CHINA
March 2021   10 9 8 7 6 5 4 3 2 1   First Edition